For Mama, determined,
courageous, and kind; the
protector and preserver of
our culture. I love you.
–RM

For Arjun, Leykh, and Zuey
–SK

About This Book

The illustrations for this book were done in mixed media and digital collage, rendered in Procreate. This book was edited by Samantha Gentry and designed by Lynn El-Roeiy and Angelie Yap with art direction from Saho Fujii. The production was supervised by Virginia Lawther, and the production editor was Annie McDonnell. The text was set in Banda Regular, and the display type is Adorn Roman.

My Diwali Light

By Raakhee Mirchandani

Art by Supriya Kelkar

Little, Brown and Company

New York Boston

Diwali is my time to shine.

From bindis and bangles to diyas and decorations, the Diwali season is all about the sparkle. And so am I!

But before I can peacock in Patiala pants or twirl in my new lehenga, I've got to get my room ready for Lakshmi Mata. Nani says when we clean our home, we remember to keep our hearts clean, too.

I throw on my best cleaning ensemble and
hope that Mama doesn't check under my bed.

"All clean, Mama!" I tell her, my stomach rumbling from the smells of Diwali filling up our apartment. All that organizing sure made me hungry.

Nani is in the kitchen frying puris that look like fluffy pillows. Papa forms perfectly round besan ladoos.

I add a pistachio to the top of each so the desserts look like they are wearing green bindis, just like me.

I've been saving my red bindi for a special occasion, and there's nothing more special than Diwali. But do I have anything to wear that matches?

Nani brought me five new outfits from India—bright blues, greens, yellows, and pinks. Some suits have embroidered flowers, and others have mirrored vests and tie-dyed skirts. I try them all on before deciding on today's party look.

We all celebrate Diwali in different ways.
My cousins buy new clothes. Dadi buys gold jewelry.

In my family, we wrap up our ladoos in fancy boxes
and deliver them to people we love.

Mama, Papa, and I hop from house to house, stopping in to see friends, sharing chikki and chai, sparklers and samosas.

I eat so many samosas at Nicky Maasi's house, I think I'm going to burst!

At Mamaji's house, I get to be the DJ,
playing all our favorite songs.

But my favorite part about Diwali
is the big party we have in our
apartment.

Papa makes the most delicious pakoras, paneer, and chaat. Mama hangs strings of marigolds and twinkling lights. Nani helps me paint diyas. She says the flame is a reminder for all of us to shine our lights brightly, to be kind, helpful, and loving.

Our friends arrive, bringing mithai and macarons, cookies and ladoos. Nani says the sweet treats remind us to speak sweetly to each other, not just on Diwali, but always.

I can barely speak with all these jalebis in my mouth!

The Bollywood beats travel down to the street,
and my friends clap loudly,
watching me show off
some new dance moves
I learned from my cousin Kiran.

Papa and I do rangoli on the floor with colored rice. He makes a paisley pattern, and I make a peace sign. Some of my friends try rangoli too, making hearts and rainbows.

"Diwali is the best when we are together," I tell my friends. I take a picture with my mind so I won't forget a single face.

Some neighbors pass by, asking us what we're celebrating, and we invite them to join us.

The more people, the brighter the light—
that's our Diwali motto.

After our guests are gone, Mama and Papa drink chai, and Nani and I sneak away to exchange presents.

I give her a bracelet I made with my best beads. I wear to sleep the necklace she gave me.

"Happy Diwali, Devi," Mama whispers when she wakes me up the next morning. It's finally here, my favorite holiday!

I give Mama and Papa big hugs and the Diwali cards I made for them at school. Papa gets glitter in his hair and Mama gets some on her eyelashes. They both shimmer like stars.

When it's time for the Diwali puja, I sit right in the front and help Papa get the thali ready.

I sprinkle the rice and the water and help shower the statues in the mandir with milk, yogurt, honey, ghee, and sugar. We offer flowers and mithai. I shake the coins. Mama sings the aarti, and I ring my bell loudly.

We all pray our own prayers, quietly whispering
words of hope from deep in our hearts.

Mama said she prayed that we are happy and healthy. Papa said he prayed for peace and happiness around the world. Nani said she prayed that we are always together on Diwali.

I pray that my Diwali light
shines all year long.

Author's Note

Diwali is the holiday that feels like it belongs to me. *My Diwali Light* tells the story of Devi, named after my grandmother, as she gets ready to celebrate Diwali *her* way. Like so many major holidays, different families and communities have their own ways of marking the season. Growing up in an immigrant Sindhi household in New Jersey, our celebration looked different than many of our friends. I made sure to include the Diwali details that always stand out for me, like the jingling of the coins during puja, or worship. My grandmother told me we jingle the coins loudly so Lakshmi, the goddess we honor during Diwali, showers our home with health and wealth.

I hear my grandmother Devi's voice throughout this story. And now that I have a family of my own, my daughter, Satya, and I have started our own Diwali tradition: a huge party where we cram as many people as possible into our apartment for food, dancing, and lots of laughs. I love celebrating Diwali, but what I love most is sharing Diwali with our friends, bringing them into our world, our apartment, and our culture. I love making it our own, creating new traditions, while also honoring the ones that have been passed down to us by our ancestors. I love knowing that all the Diwali light and sparkle isn't gone when the holiday is over: It's in the truth, kindness, and empathy we carry within us all year round. I think what I love most is imagining how all our inner lights, yours and mine, can brighten the darkest corners of the world and the gloomiest of days.

I hope when you read this book, about a time of year that is both sacred and joyous for my family and me, it sparks conversations about holidays that you celebrate and why they matter to you. Happy Diwali, friends!